Jolly Roger and the Coconuts

Story by Elsie Nelley

Illustrations by Chantal Stewart

"The fish are not here today,"
said Big Pirate.

"I can see coconuts,"
said Jolly Roger.
"Coconuts are good to eat."

"I'm very hungry,"
said Little Pirate.
"I will get us some coconuts."

"It is not safe up here," cried Little Pirate.

"Come back down," said Big Pirate. "I will get the coconuts."

"I cannot get the coconuts," shouted Big Pirate.

"Look out!

I'm coming down, too."

Jolly Roger looked at the two pirates.

"I'm not going up the tree to get the coconuts," he said. "My coat and my boots will get dirty."

"I'm hungry," said Little Pirate. "Please get us some coconuts."

"We will look after your coat and your boots," said Big Pirate.

Jolly Roger went all the way up the tree.

"Look out!" he shouted.

Splash! Splash!

Two little coconuts went into the waves.

"Thanks, Jolly Roger," said the pirates.
"We will not be hungry today."